The *Professor* Who Taught Me to L♥ve

Sejal Ruhela

 Scribe

Publisher: Inkscirbe Publishing Pvt Ltd
ISBN Number: 978-1-966421-16-0

Table of Contents

The End That Began It All

Breakups suck.

Especially when you're a teenager. It feels like your whole life is over. As if someone pressed pause on the world, just for you to cry in peace.

Same thing happened to Momo. A little lie, a small betrayal — and boom, everything collapsed. Life wasn't just sad. It was *drama-level* sad. Like movie-type sad. She cried. She shut down. She stopped talking, stopped eating, stopped going to college.

And then came anxiety. And panic attacks. The kind that made her feel like she couldn't breathe, like the room was shrinking and the walls were closing in. At one point, she genuinely believed she was going mad.

Her parents were terrified. They didn't say much. But you could see it in their eyes — they were losing their daughter. And for what? A guy who lied?

That hit her hard. That night, something snapped. She realized — okay, maybe he left. But why should she leave too? Why should her parents suffer for something they never did?

That's when the comeback began.

Slowly, she started picking herself up. Not all at once. One step at a time. One day she opened her books. One day she tied her hair properly. One day she cleaned her room. And finally, one day — she stepped back into college.

Third unit test. First day back.

She walked into the classroom like a ghost. No makeup. No chitchat. No fake smile. Just a straight face and a "don't talk to me" vibe. But of course, people *still* talked.

Because she wasn't just some random girl. She was half of the couple everyone admired. The cool one. The romantic one. The *"aww so cute"* one.

And now? The *"oh my god, what happened?"* girl.

The classroom buzzed with whispers. Some fake concern. Some nosy questions. Mostly gossip. Everyone wanted to know the story.

She ignored them all and took her seat — front bench, third row. Head down. Focused. 9:00 AM. Exam time.

One invigilator entered and began distributing sheets. The other one... was missing. Or late. Whatever.

She began writing. A girl in front of her started copying. Boldly. As if her answer sheet was public property.

She wanted to stop her. Say something. But nah — no energy. No drama.

So she looked around. Hoping the second invigilator would show up and handle it. And then... there he was.

Sitting at the back. Calm. Casual. Lavender shirt. Neckband. Clean sneakers. A white sipper in one hand, like he was there for vibes, not for invigilation.

He didn't look strict. Didn't even look like a teacher. More like someone who wandered in by mistake and decided to stay.

Their eyes met.

One solid second of eye contact. She didn't smile. He didn't blink.

She wasn't impressed. Just annoyed.

"Can't he see what's happening? That girl is copying from me!"

He saw it. Definitely. But didn't move. Didn't say a word.

She frowned. Whispered under her breath — *"Stupid invigilator. Useless."*

That was it. Nothing happened. No dramatic moment. No background music. Just one guy sitting. One girl judging. And a vibe that neither of them understood yet.

The Chomu Physics Waale Sir

Exams got over. Thank God.

After all the drama and breakdowns and that one weird invigilator staring episode — she was finally trying to get back to normal life. Like, regular college classes, bunk plans, hostel gossip... the works.

But life, as usual, had other plans.

She came back to campus, hoping for a boring day. You know, the kind where nothing happens, and the professor drones on while everyone pretends to take notes.

Instead, boom — news broke. Their physics professor had quit.

Now normally, that wouldn't bother her. She hated physics. Never understood what the hell "potential difference" had to do with real life anyway. But still — her teacher? She liked her. Sweet lady. Made zero sense while teaching, but still sweet.

So yeah, there was a weird little sadness.

And just as she was lost in that thought, someone entered the classroom.

And guess who it was? No, seriously — guess.

Yup. The same second invigilator.

The lavender-shirt guy. The Sketchers guy. The "stupid, useless invigilator" guy.

He walked in like he owned the place. At first, she was confused.

"Why is he here? Isn't his shift over?"

But then he started speaking. And it hit her like a brick.

He wasn't visiting.

He wasn't there by mistake.

He. Was. The. New. Physics. Teacher. Her jaw dropped.

Her brain couldn't process it.

Out of all the people in the world, this guy had to replace her favourite teacher? And teach *physics*? Great. Just great.

Her batchmates seemed okay with it. Apparently, some of them already knew. They smiled at him, nodded, acted normal.

But for her?

It was a tragedy.

No, worse — it was a personal attack.

Because not only had she already judged him once during the exam, now he was also taking her fav teacher's place. In her least favourite subject.

A triple threat.

In her head, there was no saving this man now. He had officially become her enemy. His face? Annoying.

His voice? Extra annoying.

His handwriting on the board? Annoying-er.

She tolerated the class like it was a punishment. And the moment the bell rang, she rushed home — rage mode activated.

And that evening? Oh boy.

She unloaded everything at home.

"There's a new teacher. Total chomu. I swear, I'm going to fail now. Physics is over for me. Career over. Life over."

Her family tried to calm her down. But nope. Not happening.

Days passed. Classes continued. He taught. She ignored. Zero eye contact. Zero communication. A cold war with no bullets.

That was the arrangement. Or so she thought.

Because fate, as usual, had other things planned.

Accused, Observed, and Something Unsaid

Time was moving forward. People were moving on. But not her. Some memories aren't just hard to forget — they dig a hole in your brain and settle there like unwanted tenants.

It had been months, but her ex still lived in her mind rent-free. And that day, she arrived at college earlier than usual — maybe hoping that silence would give her some peace.

Instead, silence made her remember everything.

She stood outside her classroom, back against the wall, eyes unfocused.

She didn't even realize how long she'd been standing there — or who all had walked past her. And that's when it happened.

A sharp voice broke the silence.

"Which department are you from? What's your name?"

She blinked — startled. A tall man in formal clothes stood in front of her, expression unreadable. She gave him a confused answer and left, not thinking much of it.

He wasn't familiar. Just some faculty, maybe. Nothing important. Or so she thought.

Hours later, her phone vibrated in the middle of class.

HOD Calling.

Weird. They *never* called during lectures. Something felt off. She went out to pick up.

"Come to my office right now," the voice said. No explanation. Just an order.

She walked in, expecting maybe some notice, some formal announcement. Instead, she was handed a verbal complaint.

"For what?"

"For not saying good morning," the HOD said bluntly. "The new Dean feels you lack basic etiquette."

For a second, everything froze.

She had never even *known* that man was the Dean. And now... a complaint? A character judgement? One tiny moment — her mind lost in pain — and suddenly, she was labelled disrespectful?

That's when something inside her cracked. This wasn't just unfair. This was personal.

She stormed back into class.

The lecture was halfway through.

Physics Sir — yeah, *that* professor — was teaching.

The moment she entered, his eyes locked onto her. She ignored him and went to her seat.

But he noticed. Of course he did.

"You look upset," he said, mid-equation. "Everything okay?" She snapped.

"Nothing's wrong."

But he didn't drop it.

He asked again. And again.

Finally, tired of pretending, she said it.

"The Dean filed a complaint. Said I don't have etiquette. Just because I didn't say good morning." She expected him to say something comforting. Or maybe just nod.

Instead, he went silent. His expression changed — not pity, not concern. Something else. Something unreadable.

"Forget it," she mumbled. "Let's just drop it."

The lecture ended, but he didn't pack up like usual.

He left — quickly, quietly — and didn't return for the next class. What she didn't know was that he had gone straight to the Dean's office. No one knew what was said in that room.

But things changed.

By lunch, the Dean himself came to her.

"I'm sorry," he said. "I misunderstood. You were probably... dealing with something. I shouldn't have judged."

She said nothing. Just nodded. Still stunned. But her mind was somewhere else now.

How did the Dean change his mind so fast?

He seemed so sure a few hours ago.

What exactly had happened in that office?

Later, when Physics Sir returned to class, he looked at her with that same unreadable calm. "Everything okay now?" he asked softly.

She nodded again.

"You were right," he added. "It wasn't your fault."

And just for a second — only a second — she wondered:

Was he just a teacher? Or was he... something more?

Because the way he noticed, the way he reacted, and the way he convinced the Dean to apologize — none of it was normal.

There was something he wasn't saying.

And she could feel it in the silence between his words.

The Lunchbox That Changed Everything

In a world full of chaos and constant noise, he was the only one who understood her silence—no questions, no judgments, just quiet acceptance. Maybe... just maybe, she had been wrong about the professor. Maybe he wasn't the villain she had painted in my head.

Days passed. The irritation she once felt started fading, and didn't even realize when. It was **7th May**. The first time she texted him.

Not for flirting, okay? Just to ask the syllabus.

He replied hours later. After being online... *constantly*. She could see his "last seen," his green dot, but her message? Completely ignored. When he finally replied, she stared at the screen.

"Arrogant," she whispered to herself.

But no. She had promised myself not to judge him again. So... breathe in, breathe out, and move on.

Time passed. Things were stable. Normal. And then, one day, she saw him again—in a way she hadn't before.

He was at the cafeteria. Ordering something. Just as he finished eating, another faculty member handed him a home-cooked lunchbox. And guess what? He didn't even hesitate—opened it, tore off two pieces of roti, and finished it in minutes.

Momo stood there, watching. Not stalking—just... observing. And in that moment, she realized something.

He wasn't just eating. He was *savouring*. The man was in love—with food.

And she had finally found the perfect way to say thank you. Not with words. But with something he truly valued.

Food.

There was just one problem. she didn't know how to cook.

But YouTube exists for a reason, right?

Next morning, Momo woke up at 4. Searched for recipes. Watched five to seven videos. Finally figured out what to make and how. Burnt her finger once. Dropped a spoon twice. But somehow... she did it.

Packed everything. Took a deep breath. And went to college.

Now, in our class, there's always that one person who brings lunch for everyone. That's her. Because she is a day scholar. But today... no one else mattered.

She had cooked only for him.

So when her friends asked, "Lunch kya banaya?" She lied. "Didn't bring today."

At lunchtime, Momo called him. "Where are you?" she asked. "Why?" he replied.

"I brought lunch for you. Come take it." There was silence on the other end. "For... me?" His voice held disbelief.

"Yes," she said flatly. "Or should I give it to someone else?" "NO!" he almost shouted.

She smiled. Left the lunch in his lab and walked back to class. He was still busy, but just minutes later, she saw him walking toward the classroom.

Holding the lunchbox.

He didn't even wait. He opened it right there. His eyes sparkled.

Chhole puri.

Coincidence? Maybe. Or maybe not. Because it turned out to be his favourite.
He called her while eating. Thanked her. Praised the taste. Admired the effort. And then came the inevitable question.
"But... why did you cook for me?"
She said nothing. Smiled quietly. He asked again.
Still silence.
Because she had no answer. Or maybe... she wasn't ready to say it out loud yet.

The Knock That Changed Everything

Although the lunch was finished, the professor's curiosity was far from satisfied. His stomach might have been full, but his mind? Restless. Doubts, questions, and a strange urge to figure out what exactly was running inside Momo's head—it all started from there. That was when he began observing her... more than usual.

Momo, on the other hand, was often lost in her own world, drifting between silence and shadows. She didn't laugh with others, didn't hang out after lectures, never really blended in. The professor, being the mature and composed person he was, didn't just let it slide. He quietly asked around— classmates, seniors, anyone who might know something.

That's when he found out about the breakup.

After lectures, while everyone left for the canteen or hostel, Momo stayed behind. Same desk. Same corner. Same silence. She would scribble her assignments, eventually doze off over her notebooks, the weight of heartbreak pressing against her eyes.

One day, he was passing by her class. The corridor echoed with emptiness. Just as he was about to walk away, he paused. The lights were still on.

Peeking inside, he saw her.

Momo. Head down on a notebook. Hair falling over her face. Pen loosely held in one hand. A tired mess of strength and pain.

He stepped in, quietly. For a moment, he didn't say anything. Just looked at her. Thought to himself—*She doesn't deserve this.*

Then he noticed something else—a physics equation on her notebook. Completely wrong. Smiling slightly, he corrected it. Gently knocked on the desk.

"Hey, wake up. It's 5:00. Your bus is waiting. You'll miss it. Hurry up!"

Startled, Momo stood up, grabbed her things, and ran out. It took a few seconds to register what had just happened. *Did he come looking for me? How did he even know I was in class? And I didn't even say thank you...*

But there was no time. The bus was about to leave. Questions had to wait.

That night, something kept circling her thoughts. Over and over again—*Was he actually... searching for me?*

And well, girls know. Every girl does. When a guy starts helping without any reason, looks at you differently, remembers the small things—it means only one thing: *He has a crush on you.*

Momo started smiling at that thought. A little happy. A little embarrassed. But the real embarrassment... was yet to come.

The next day, during lunch, he called her. Asked her to come to the lab. She went—along with a friend, just in case.

What happened next? A total plot twist.

He took them to the **Agricultural Department**. Yes, out of all places—vegetables, mud, and greenhouses.

Not exactly the "romantic setup" Momo had in mind.

He walked slowly, hands behind his back, looking at the plants like they were some kind of
masterpiece. Meanwhile, Momo and her friend exchanged confused glances, wondering what on earth was happening.

"What do you observe in this?" he asked.

Momo stared blankly. Then smiled nervously. "Nothing." He laughed softly.

"I don't know you that well, Momo," he said, "but I can sense things. Your vibe? It's chill. Positive. Full of motivation. But right now, what I'm seeing doesn't match that at all. Just like how you're not

observing anything in these vegetables... I can't find *you* in you." Silence.

"Am I wrong?" he asked.

Momo didn't speak. Couldn't speak.

"I know about your breakup," he continued. "It's not easy. I get it. But tell me something... is it the end of your life?"

He paused, turned to her slowly. "You've known him for what... six months? And for that, you're breaking down this much?"

Momo's eyes widened. *How does he know?* The embarrassment? Real. But what hit harder was what he said next.

"I had a breakup too," he said, calm but a little distant. "Ten years. Ten long years. And it ended a few months ago."

Momo looked up, shocked.

"But here I am—smiling, teaching, eating, living. Yes, it hurts. But life doesn't stop, Momo. Don't lock yourself in. Explore who you are. Let the past go. This pain isn't your identity."

And just like that, the conversation ended.

"Okay, back to class. I've got a lecture," he said, laughing lightly.

Momo watched him walk away. Something had shifted inside her. That night, she didn't overthink. She just sent a message.

"Thank you."

And that... was the moment the never-ending story began—at least, from Momo's side.

The Thunder Before Bloom

It wasn't just a thank you message—it was the ignition switch. The first real spark between Momo and the professor. From that one text, something subtle yet powerful began. Momo didn't just feel gratitude anymore. She felt warmth. A comfort she hadn't known since her heart had been broken.

And him? Well, he didn't say much. But something in his responses... something hinted he had started feeling special too. Yet he hid it, buried it beneath layers of maturity and professionalism.

He knew. Of course, he knew. A man like him, composed and observant, could read more from

silence than words. He could see the eagerness in Momo's excuses—questions that weren't really questions, doubts that didn't need answers, sudden sick leaves just to get a "why" from him. He noticed. But he acted like he didn't.

Momo wasn't giving up, though. Her messages came like light rain—soft but persistent. Seven, sometimes eight, before one dry response came in. Or sometimes, silence. Pure ignorance, as if he'd mastered the art of invisibility.

One rainy afternoon, while everyone stood huddled at the bus stop, laughing and enjoying the

drizzle, Momo stood quietly among them. Her gaze was fixed on the wet sky, lost in thought, when suddenly, a low, soft voice brushed her ear.

"Hii..."

She turned with a start. "Oh, you?" she said, surprised.

"So, you still know me. I thought I was long forgotten," he said with a teasing smile. "Why would I forget you?" she asked.

"Well, you sent 7-8 messages. I replied... once." "Exactly," she said, arms folded.

He laughed, then leaned a little. 50 rehte hai," he whispered, and walked away, leaving her stunned and smiling.

That moment told her something: *this is not going to be easy.* But it was worth trying.

A few days later, Momo executed a plan. She knew he boarded the college bus midway, and sometimes didn't get a seat. She decided to save the front one for him—the seat near the driver, his favorite.

She placed her bag on the seat early in the morning and waited. As expected, he entered the bus, saw the bag, and asked the driver, "Kisi ka hai yeh?"

The driver shrugged. He sat down. Plan successful. But... she never got the chance to tell him. As the bus halted at the college gate, he got off in a hurry. Momo watched helplessly. *Ugh, at least say thanks!* she thought.

That evening, she texted him:

"You know that seat you sat on today? I saved it for you. And you didn't even thank me."

The reply came:

"Oh, were you also in the bus? I didn't notice. But... thank you."

Didn't notice? Momo stared at the screen. *You're the only reason I got on that bus early today!*

Still, she stayed strong.

Later, with a fabricated doubt in physics (a subject she never even liked), she went to his lab. He was alone, engrossed in some work, but when he saw her, he packed everything up just to help.

Just the two of them. Silence wrapped around the lab like a warm quilt. Only his voice echoed, slow and soothing, explaining some random theory she wasn't even trying to understand. Momo was watching his face more than the formulas. His eyes. His calm. That comforting aura. She forgot the chapter, forgot the world.

He paused, noticing her gaze. "You okay?" he asked.

"Yes, yes! Of course," she said, blinking rapidly. "I just... I don't think physics is for me. But thank you!" she added quickly, scooping her books and rushing out, cheeks burning.

Outside, adjusting her hair, trying to compose herself, she stopped.

Him.

Her ex.

Coming from the other side, laughing on a call, carefree, as if the world hadn't collapsed for someone once because of him.

Her breath shortened. Eyes welled up. She stepped back. Re-entered the lab. He noticed. "What happened?"

She didn't answer.

He gently insisted. After ten silent minutes, she whispered, "My ex. Outside."

He checked. Came back. Sat beside her. Handed her water. "It's okay. You're safe. I'm here. I won't let anything happen to you, not now, not ever. Trust me."

He placed his hand softly on her head. A gentle touch. The kind that doesn't ask for permission. Just heals.

Momo looked into his eyes. And something changed. He stood up again, checked outside, then came back. "He's gone. You'll sit here for a while. I'll be back."

Ten minutes later, he returned—with Momo's bag. He had packed up her stuff from the classroom. She smiled. Of course, she did.

They walked together toward the bus and sat next to each other. The journey was calm, until he broke the silence.

"What do you like to eat?"

She turned, surprised. "White sauce pasta." "Ahh, pasta. I love it too," he said, eyes twinkling.

He spoke more that evening—about food, about memories, about random things. And when it was time to part, he got off the bus, waved, and said, "Bye. Take care."

Momo leaned back, heart full. But her phone buzzed.

His name. A call.

"Umm... just let me know when you reach home. Message or call, okay? And... don't overthink." She smiled, whispered back, "Okay... I'll let you know. Thank you. Bye."

He paused. "Umm... or if you want to stay on call till you reach... I don't mind. We can talk..." Her lips curled into a shy smile. And that was it.

The day she stopped chasing comfort from the past. And started walking slowly toward something new. Something real. Something that wasn't a dream anymore.

The Smile That Made Her Stay

That night, the call wasn't just a call—it was comfort. We talked about random stuff, laughed a little, teased a lot. And then, without thinking twice, she gave him a cute little pet name—Dudu. With a soft laugh, he accepted it. Not a single question, not a second thought. Just a sweet, simple acceptance... like he liked it.

Somewhere between the smiles, she gathered the courage to speak what had been pinching me inside.

"You always ignored me, na? I used to wait for you every morning just to wish you a simple good morning. You never looked at me..."

There was a pause. A deep one.

"I'm sorry," he said slowly, "I didn't mean to ignore you. I never wanted to hurt you. But yeah... maybe I did disappoint you without realizing. I'm really sorry, Momo."

She reached home while they were still talking. "Ohh... so soon?" he said, his voice dropping a little. "Yeah, I've reached."

"Okay... then take rest. And if you ever feel like talking... don't forget, I'm here."

That one line... worked like magic. Like a warm hug on a cold day. She slept so peacefully that night— no fear, no ache, no past haunting me.

Next morning, he entered the bus—not looking for a seat, but for momo. He found her, waved, and smiled. And that was it.

Her whole day lit up with just that one smile.

He sat at the front, and she could clearly see his face in the bus mirror. He looked lost in thoughts. She craved his attention. So she texted—

"Itni dhyaan se window glass ko dekhoge toh toot hi jaayega."

He read it through the notification, smiled softly—yeah, she noticed. But the next moment, he acted like he never saw anything.

So she kept poking.

"Aree abhi bhi ruke nahi? Ruk jao... kya ho gaya? Todh kar hi manoge?"

She kept texting, one after another, and he kept reading, one after another. And then? Pretend game on. Total teacher mode. After reaching college, he finally replied—"Sudhar jao."

She smiled like an idiot. Blushed even harder. Who cared about boring physics lectures now? All she did was watch him secretly... while he tried his best to ignore me.

By evening, our new routine kicked in. Daily messages. Sharing how the day went, what we ate, what we felt, random emotions, silly jokes. Slowly, she forgot her pain. Slowly, she forgot everything. It was just... him.

But my past? It had different plans. It came crawling back again. 4th June. She came home from college, scrolling through Instagram like always. And then... boom. A post from her cousin's story—cousin and her ex. Romantic pose, lovey-dovey caption, slow song

playing in the background. Private story. Her heart stopped. She texted her.

"What are you doing with him? He's engaged! That's why we broke up." She was confused. "Engaged? What? He never told me anything like that!" She added him in a group chat with both of us.

"What is Momo saying? Is this true? Are you engaged with someone else?"

At first, silence. Then, after a lot of pushing, he said it—

"No, I'm not engaged. I lied to her. I wanted to end things with her... I love you."

Shattered.
Again.
She didn't know what to do. She didn't even think. She just... messaged Dudu and started crying. Didn't tell him what happened. Just kept crying. He panicked.
He called. She declined.
He called again. She declined again.
Again and again—until finally, she picked up. Stayed silent. And then he said, softly—

"What happened, Momo? Tell me."

And she cried. She told him everything. He didn't know how to react. But he didn't rush. First, he calmed me down. Slowly, gently. Then, to distract me, he shared his first meeting with his ex—filmy stuff, like a movie plot. And while listening, like a child holding onto a fairy tale, she fell asleep.
She woke up at 11:52 PM.
His birthday was in 8 minutes. At 12, she called.

"Happy Birthday, Dudu."

"Thank you..." came his sleepy voice.

Next morning, he had to leave for Kolkata. As lazy as he is during weekends, he turns into a machine on working days. But to make sure he doesn't miss his bus, she called him to wake him up.

He greeted me with—

"Good morning. You didn't even wish me Happy Birthday, so bad of you."

She was shocked.

"What?! I called you at 12!"

"Oh... really? I don't remember anything. I was dead tired and sleepy," he said, laughing.

Later, she went to see him off. She had bike with her "Ride it," he said.

"I only ride it when I'm alone," she smiled.

He looked into my eyes, said nothing, and then—

"I trust you. You won't let me fall. Just ride slowly, I'm here."

And just like that, he sat behind me. Quietly. Calmly. Trusting me completely.

They reached the bus stand. She heart didn't want him to go. He knew that. Saw it in her eyes. So he missed 4–5 buses, one after another. Just stood there. No rush.

Then finally, when a bus came and he stepped forward, he

turned back. She was looking at the bus, and he...

He gave me a **side hug**. Quick, soft, silent. Ran to the bus.

Didn't look back.

He knew... if he looked back, she might cry. So instead, he called
me—

"Hey, I'm in the **bus** now. You should go home too."

They stayed on the call for a while. No words. Just breathing.
And then... she rode back.

Not alone.

Never again alone.

"Distance That Drew Us Closer"

Momo and Dudu had now slipped into a rhythm—a comforting routine where they stayed connected through every little movement of their day. A "Have you reached?" from one, a quick "Yes, just now" from the other, followed by a few stolen moments of conversation. Short chats, stolen in between college, work, or travel, had now become the threads of a growing bond.

The next morning brought a little twist to Momo's usual routine—there was a wedding in her family, and she had to travel to Ghaziabad. But what truly excited her wasn't the wedding or the dresses, it was the fact that she'd be passing through Noida. She knew it was close to Dudu's home. And like an innocent child excited to be near someone they admire, she messaged him:

"I'm going to Ghaziabad, through Noida. Was looking for your house from the car window, but sadly... couldn't spot it."

That was enough to spark Dudu's reaction. Within seconds, her phone rang.

"Where are you? I'm coming!"

he said excitedly.

"Don't be crazy! I'm with my family. Please don't," she replied, half laughing, half panicked. "It's just 15 minutes from my home, at least send me the location!"

But she didn't. Not because she didn't want to see him, but because sometimes... feelings are too fragile to face in public.

Later that day, when Momo was struggling with salon bookings and ride arrangements in the middle of all the wedding chaos, it was Dudu who stepped in—without even being asked. He booked her a salon, arranged a cab, and made sure everything went smoothly.

From a distance, he became her comfort zone.

That evening, Momo did a video call just to show him her final look. The moment he picked up, his eyes widened, and a soft gasp left his lips.

"Oh my God... Momo, you look *beautiful*..." he whispered.

She blushed, eyes twinkling with pride and shyness. It was a moment she didn't want to end.

Even though they were cities apart, the distance only seemed to bring them emotionally closer. Their conversations deepened. From silly teasing to silent comfort, everything felt... right.

One night, while on a long call, Momo broke down.

"I don't think I'm a good girl, Dudu," she said in a low, shaken voice. "I'm not smart, not beautiful, not even confident. I don't even know how to talk properly. I'm not brilliant like others... I'm just... plain me."

There was silence for a second. Then a soft chuckle.

"What? Momo, are you even listening to yourself? You're the most beautiful, soft-hearted, positive, charming girl I've ever

31

met. And yes, you are brilliant. You just don't know it yet."

She stayed silent, eyes stinging.

"You've been through pain, I know. But don't let that define your worth. You're more than what the past did to you. And listen to me carefully—one day, you'll shine so bright that even the stars will look at you and smile. And when that happens, I'll be standing right there, proud of you."

Momo didn't respond. But those words stayed with her.

Because for the first time in her life... someone believed in her more than she believed in herself. And that made all the difference.

Strings That Pulled the Distance Closer

Momo was tired. Tired of functions, forced smiles, fake compliments, and the endless chaos of relatives at the wedding in Ghaziabad. Everyone was busy showing off clothes and jewellery; no one noticed the girl hiding behind a smile, faking a laugh, secretly wishing for one hug of comfort.

Amid all that noise, one name echoed in her mind—**Dudu**.

Though miles away, he somehow felt closer than everyone around. She had told him she wouldn't be able to talk much. Family restrictions. But Dudu didn't complain. Instead, he quietly ensured

everything went smoothly for her—booked a cab, arranged a salon appointment, and made sure she looked perfect for the wedding she didn't care about.

That night, Momo finally stepped out of the hall and sat alone near the balcony railing, scrolling through her phone. A message popped up.

Dudu: "Got 10 mins for your Dudu?"

Momo smiled. Her fingers trembled slightly as she hit the video call button. His face appeared—calm, tired, but glowing with warmth.

"Hi **Momo**."

His voice hit like a lullaby.

And just like that, the walls crumbled.

Tears welled up in her eyes.

"I feel invisible here... like I don't belong." Dudu didn't interrupt. He just listened.

"I'm not pretty like my cousins. I don't know how to pose for pictures or charm people. Everyone just... skips over me."

"But I never did, Momo."

His voice was firm. Gentle, but firm.

"You're beautiful in ways they'll never understand. You light up when you talk about the things you love—food, music, chai. That's the kind of beauty people remember."

There was silence. Heavy, healing silence. "You're **brilliant, you know that?**" he continued.

"You learn fast, feel deeply, love truly. You're not made for shallow things." Momo's lips quivered. "But I don't even know what I'm good at... I feel useless." "Then let's find out together." That night, Dudu didn't just comfort her—he gave her a mirror to see herself differently. And so began a quiet transformation. She started doodling on hotel napkins. Tried sketching when no one was looking. Even wrote a short poem on her phone titled *"Invisible Firefly."* She didn't show it to anyone. Except Dudu. His reply?

"You just drew your soul in words. Keep going." That one line lit something inside her.

Maybe she wasn't meant to blend in.

Maybe she was born to create something only she could.

And for the first time, Momo didn't cry herself to sleep. She fell asleep with her phone in hand, still connected to Dudu, her screen glowing softly as he watched over her dreams.

A Thousand Unsayable Things

Returning from Ghaziabad, Momo was no longer the same girl who had left for the wedding. Something inside her had shifted. Something soft, warm, and quietly powerful.

She had started scribbling more, sketching random faces, writing bits of poetry that didn't rhyme but somehow made perfect sense to her. And every little thing she created—she sent it to only one

person. Dudu.

He responded to each with the care of someone holding a fragile bird. "You've got magic in your fingers."

"This sketch looks like it's breathing." "Your poetry makes silence speak."

Their chats had no filter, no show-off, no pressure. It was comfort. It was home.

Late-night calls became their daily ritual. It started with random topics—weather, food, assignments—but always ended with something personal.

"What's your happiest memory?" "What do you fear the most?" "What would you do if you weren't afraid?"

Dudu always answered honestly. Momo always hesitated, then opened up.

And one night, while talking about childhood dreams, Dudu said softly, "Sometimes, I wish I had someone who understood me without explanations."

Momo stayed quiet. And he added,

"But now I feel like I do."

She didn't know what to say. Her heart thudded loud enough to fill the silence. But she didn't need to say anything. Some connections don't need validation.

One evening, Dudu didn't message.

Momo kept checking her phone every ten minutes. She told herself to focus on studies. She told herself it was nothing. But her heart didn't listen.

Hours passed. Midnight hit. And finally—*ding.*

Dudu: "Sorry, Momo. A lot going on. I didn't want to dump my mess on you." Her fingers flew across the screen.

"You're allowed to lean on me too, Dudu." He replied after a pause:

"I'm still figuring out how to do that."

She didn't push him. She just sent a simple message:

"I'm here. No rush. No pressure."

That night, Dudu sent her a voice note. He spoke slowly, tiredly, but with trust.

"Some days I feel like I have to carry the world. But when I talk to you... it feels lighter."

Momo closed her eyes and replayed that message five times. She wanted to bottle that feeling forever.

One morning, she saw her phone light up at 6:00 a.m.

Dudu: "Wake up, sunshine. I dreamt of you last night."

Her heart fluttered like a teenage diary page. She replied,

"Was it romantic or tragic?"

Dudu: "Neither. Just real. You were dancing in the rain. Happy. Wild. Free." She stared at the screen.

For the first time, she wished the dream was true.

And for the first time, she wondered if this thing between them was slowly turning into something else. Something more.

But love? No. Not yet.

At least, not the kind they could name.

It was still growing—like a secret garden only they could enter.

Almost Love

Momo had started to smile without reason.

She would catch herself humming while brushing her hair, sketching while lost in thoughts, laughing at texts that weren't even meant to be funny. And it was always him—Dudu.

He was now a permanent part of her days and nights. Like a bookmark in her story, saving her place even when life got chaotic.

One evening, Dudu texted:

"Do you ever think we met for a reason?" The question caught her off guard. "What do you mean?" she replied.

"I don't know. It just feels like... the universe planned it. Like I was supposed to meet you. At that time. In that way."

Momo didn't reply for a full minute. Then finally typed:

"Maybe we both were broken in different ways. And healing needed a partner." Dudu sent a voice note.

His voice was quiet, almost trembling.

"I didn't believe in destiny, you know. But then you happened. And suddenly... I started questioning everything I thought I knew."

Momo lay still, her phone resting on her chest, her eyes moist. Was it love? Or the preface to love? She didn't know. But she knew it was real.

The next week was Dudu's off from college. He had gone to his hometown. The calls were less, the texts delayed.

Momo felt the gap like a missing rib.

She waited patiently, but one night she gave in and sent:

"I miss you more than I should." And this time, his reply was quick.

"I miss you too, Momo. More than I want to admit."

She read that again and again. Saved it. Read it once more. Then whispered to herself, *"Is this how love feels when it's still shy?"*

One day, Dudu sent a message:

"I want to see you."

"Now?" she asked, heart racing.

"No. I mean... someday. Somewhere peaceful. No rush. Just us. Talking. Breathing."

And that night, for the first time ever, Momo fell asleep smiling with her phone in her hand.

When Dudu returned to college, something had changed. He looked at her longer.

He spoke softer.

He stood a little closer.

Momo felt it all. And maybe... he did too.

One afternoon, as they stood by the college stairs, watching the sky slowly turn golden, Momo whispered,

"You know what scares me?" "Hmm?"

"The thought that all this... might end someday."

Dudu didn't answer right away. He stared at the horizon. Then turned to her and said,

"Some things don't end, Momo. They just change form. But feelings... real ones... they always find a way back."

And in that moment, Momo knew—this wasn't just a phase. It was *almost* love.

Not spoken yet. Not confessed.

But deeply, undeniably, there.

The First Touch

Momo had always been awkward with physical affection. Hugs made her nervous, holding hands felt too intimate, and proximity? That was a whole other storm.

But with Dudu, it was different. Not easier—but safer.

They weren't dating. They hadn't said "I love you." There were no labels. Just... feelings. Unspoken. Loud. Constant.

One morning, it rained.

Not the kind of rain that makes you run for shelter—but the soft, drizzling kind. The kind that slows the world down.

They were walking through the college garden, both holding their umbrellas, talking about nothing and everything.

Suddenly, Dudu's umbrella flipped inside out with a strong gust. Momo laughed. A full, head-thrown-back kind of laugh. And before she could react, Dudu reached out—

And held her hand.

No words. Just fingers intertwining like it was the most natural thing in the world.

Momo froze. Her skin burned where he touched her. Her heart pounded like a drumroll waiting for something dramatic to happen.

But nothing did.

And that was the drama.

They just walked like that. Hand in hand. In the rain. Silent. She didn't pull away.

He didn't tighten his grip.

It was soft. Light. But heavy with meaning. After a few minutes, Dudu said,

"You feel real." Momo looked at him.

"What do you mean?"

"I mean... sometimes I think I imagined you. That maybe I made you up because I needed someone so badly."

She smiled.

"You didn't imagine me. I'm right here. Holding your hand."

"Yeah. And I hope you never let go."

That night, they didn't talk much. Just a few texts. Dudu: "I still feel your fingers in mine."

Momo: "I still feel my heartbeat in my throat."

The next day, they didn't touch at all.

But the distance between them had changed forever.

And Momo realized... the first touch isn't always about the body.

Sometimes, it's about the soul finally finding a place to rest.

The Confession Without Saying It

Days passed after the hand-holding moment, but something had shifted. They didn't talk about it. They didn't need to.

Momo found herself smiling more. Waiting for his texts. Replaying his voice notes. Checking her phone like it was a lifeline.

And Dudu? He wasn't hiding anymore. His eyes lingered longer. His voice softened when he spoke to her. He noticed everything—her mood swings, her silence, her fake smiles.

One evening, Dudu messaged her,

"Come to the terrace. I want to show you something." She climbed the stairs quickly, confused, curious.

He stood there, holding two kulfis.

"You said you missed your childhood. So here. This is what mine tasted like."

She laughed, took the kulfi, and sat beside him. They didn't talk for a while. Just sat under the sky, letting the wind wrap around them like a blanket.

Then Dudu turned to her and asked gently, "Why are you always so scared?"

Momo looked at him, startled. "What do you mean?"

"You smile, but you flinch when someone gets close. You laugh, but your eyes always look like they're searching for a way out."

She looked down. Her kulfi started melting.

"Because everyone who said they loved me... eventually left."

Dudu didn't say anything for a few seconds. Then he said: "Then let me be the first one who doesn't."

She looked up. Right into his eyes.

He didn't say "I love you." She didn't either.

But somehow, they both heard it loud and clear.

The sky seemed to lean in. The world slowed down. "I don't know what this is," Momo whispered.

"I don't know how to trust it."

"You don't have to," he replied.

"Just don't run away. That's all I ask." She nodded slowly.

They didn't touch. Didn't hug. Didn't kiss.

But that night, when Momo lay in bed, she texted him: "I didn't run today. That's a start, right?"

Dudu: "That's everything."

Jealousy in Silence

Days passed, and the bond that had once felt like magic started to feel... different. Not broken—just tangled. Momo, wrapped up in the chaos of college, family, and herself, didn't notice the silence growing between them. It wasn't loud, it wasn't angry. It was the kind of quiet that creeps in when someone starts needing more and asking less.

Dudu, the man who had always stood calm and tall, found himself shifting. Restless. He was never one to crave attention, but with Momo, he wanted it. Not all of it—but enough to feel seen. And lately, he felt like a background character in a story he'd once written.

He watched her laugh with friends, stay online but not reply, miss calls with reasons like *"I slept off, sorry!"*—and each time, he smiled and said, "It's okay." But it wasn't. Not really.

Momo, on the other hand, didn't notice the shift in his eyes. She was too caught up in trying to balance everything—college, assignments, a thousand expectations. She was still the same, but her focus had drifted. She'd started giving her energy to the world again, assuming Dudu would always be there.

Until one evening, while scrolling through her gallery, Dudu saw a selfie Momo had posted with a classmate. Just a normal photo, just a smile—but something twisted inside him. Not because of the boy, but because he couldn't remember the last time she smiled like that for *him*.

He didn't mention it. Of course, he didn't. He wasn't the

possessive type. But that night, when Momo casually texted, *"Busy day! What about you?"*—he replied a little late and a little short. And Momo noticed.

She asked, *"Are you okay?"*

And he just typed, *"Yeah, just tired."*

But his heart whispered a truth his fingers wouldn't type: *"I miss when I was your safe space, not just a name on your notification bar."*

The Storm That Spoke

The silence was no longer peaceful—it had weight. Momo began to feel it too. Dudu's messages had become shorter, his responses slower, and his voice on calls—quieter. It wasn't his usual calm. It was distant. And though he said nothing, Momo could sense everything.

One evening, while sitting on her rooftop, the stars above and confusion within, she decided to call him.

"Hello," he said, voice low.

"Hi... what's wrong, Dudu?" she asked, not dancing around it anymore. "Nothing. Just tired," he said again.

"Don't lie. Not to me," she said softly.

There was silence on the line, but a storm behind it. And then, slowly, he spoke.

"I just..." He paused, searching for the right words. "I don't want to fight for your attention, Momo. I never wanted to be someone who needs to be reassured every day. But lately, I feel like... I don't matter like I used to."

Momo's heart dropped. It wasn't anger. It wasn't jealousy. It was hurt. And that made it worse.

"I didn't realise I was making you feel this way," she whispered.

"I've just been caught up with everything and I—"

"I know," he cut in gently. "And I'm proud of you for managing it all. But don't forget, even the strongest people need to be reminded that they're loved... especially when they start doubting it."

Momo closed her eyes, guilt washing over her.

"You're not just someone I care about, Dudu," she said, voice cracking. "You're the only person who makes me feel like I'm enough. And I'm sorry if I made you feel any less."

There was a pause. Then, he sighed, a softer one this time. "I just missed us. That's all."

A small tear slid down Momo's cheek. "Then let's find us again."

And from that night, they did. Not with grand gestures or dramatic promises—but with the little things. A goodnight call. A midday meme. A random "I miss you" text. They stitched the gap with consistency and care.

Because love, they realized, isn't just fireworks. Sometimes, it's just choosing each other. Again. And again. Even in the quiet.

The Unseen Visitor

Momo's semester exams were just around the corner, and the air in her room felt heavier than usual. Books piled up like mountains, sticky notes on every corner, and her brain? A chaos of dates, theories, and anxiety.

Sleep became a luxury. Food—skipped. Calls with Dudu? Short and scattered. He noticed. Of course, he did.

"You need to breathe, Momo," he told her one night. "You're burning out."

"I don't have time to breathe," she snapped unintentionally. "I need to finish this syllabus first." There was a pause. Not of offense, but understanding.

"Okay," he said. "But at least eat something. And sleep. Promise me that?" She didn't reply. Just stared at her screen, heart pounding.

The next morning, a knock echoed at her door. Her roommate opened it.

"Delivery for Momo."

It was a small food parcel—her favourite paneer wrap and a cup of cold coffee. Taped on top was a note in Dudu's handwriting:
"Since you won't feed yourself, let me. Eat. Now. Or I'll send a full thali next time."

Momo blinked back a tear. He was far, yet so near. And that wasn't all.

Two days later, in the middle of her revision, she got another knock. This time, it wasn't food.

It was *him*.

Dudu stood there, in a simple shirt, holding a brown paper bag. Inside it were chocolates, sticky notes with tiny motivational quotes, and her favorite black gel pen.

"You're kidding me," she whispered, eyes wide. "You came all the way?" He smiled, a little tired but happy. "I told you... you're not alone in this." She hugged him tightly, tears finally falling.

They didn't talk much that day. He sat beside her while she revised. He didn't distract. He didn't interfere. He was just there. Like a silent promise.

That night, as he left, he looked at her and said, "No matter what your result says... you're already my topper."

Her heart melted. Not because he called her brilliant. But because he showed up when she needed someone the most.

The Exam Day

The sun rose on exam day like a spotlight on stage—harsh, bright, and unforgiving.

Momo woke up early, nerves already twisting in her stomach. Her notes were scattered all over the bed, and highlighters marked everything—except peace of mind.

She got dressed in silence. Hair tied up, minimal makeup, and eyes shadowed with stress. As she slung her bag over her shoulder, her phone buzzed.

Dudu: *"You've got this, Momo. Don't panic. Read carefully. And smile—it suits you."*

She smiled. Just a little.

At the exam center, the air was buzzing with panic and prayers. Momo stood outside the hall, flipping through notes, when her heart stopped.

There he was.

Dudu.

In formal attire, holding an invigilation file, scanning the crowd. Her mind froze.

He was invigilating *her* room.

Their eyes met. He blinked once, lips twitching like he wanted to smile but wouldn't—not here, not now.

Momo panicked. Her hands went cold. How could she write with him walking around? She entered the hall with trembling steps, praying he wouldn't come near her.

But destiny had other plans.

He walked past her once, then again. His scent—familiar and calming—broke her focus. Halfway through the exam, her pen slipped. It fell with a soft *thud*.

Before she could pick it up, a hand reached down. *His* hand. Their fingers brushed.

He didn't look at her. He just placed the pen gently and walked on. Her heart? It ran a marathon.

Somehow, she wrote the paper. Not perfect, not terrible. Just okay.

After the bell rang and the chaos of chairs scraping filled the room, Momo slowly packed her things. She stepped outside, expecting to leave quietly, but a familiar voice stopped her.

"Wait."

She turned.

Dudu was leaning against a pillar, arms crossed, a slight smile tugging at his lips. "You survived."

"I did," she whispered.

He walked closer, eyes softening. "I was worried I'd distract you." "You did."

He laughed, low and genuine. "Sorry, Miss Momo."

She looked at him for a second. Then reached into her bag, pulled out a tiny note she'd written during the break.

She handed it to him silently.

"Thanks for believing in me when I didn't believe in myself."

His eyes scanned it. And for a second, the tough teacher faded. He became Dudu again—her Dudu. "I always will," he said.

And just like that, a new memory was added to their story.

The Result of Us

The results were just a few clicks away. And yet, Momo's fingers hovered over the keyboard like it was a bomb.

The night before, she had barely slept. Her thoughts tangled between exam memories, Dudu's lingering glance, and the haunting fear of failure.

She stared at the laptop screen, heart pounding louder than the fan above her.

Enter Roll Number.

She typed. Hesitated. Then clicked.

"Congratulations! You've passed with distinction."

Tears spilled—unexpected, unfiltered, and full of disbelief. She had done it. After everything. After the mess, the breakdowns, the pain—she had made it.

Her phone vibrated.

Dudu: *"Checked?"*

She typed with shaky fingers.

Momo: *"I passed."*

A pause.

Dudu: *"I knew you would. You never saw what I saw in you."*

She wanted to cry again. Instead, she typed:

Momo: *"Thank you... for everything. I don't know if I deserved this much belief."*

Dudu: *"No, you don't deserve belief. You deserve the world, Momo."*

Later that evening, she got a voice note.

His voice was calm, proud, a little emotional. "You proved everyone wrong, including yourself. I can't celebrate with you in person today, but someday I will. And when I do, we'll celebrate more than a result. We'll celebrate you."

She hugged her phone to her chest like it was him. That night, they had a call.

Longer than usual. No formalities. Just two souls breathing in each other's success. Momo talked about how scared she was. How at one point, she felt like dropping everything.

Dudu listened, then simply said, "I'm proud of you. But more than that, I'm proud of the version of you that didn't give up."

There was silence.

Then Momo whispered, "Promise me you'll always remind me of my worth when I forget." His reply came without hesitation. "I promise. But only if you promise to start believing it on your own someday."

And that night, for the first time, Momo didn't sleep with anxiety. She slept with peace—and a tiny dream tucked in the corner of her heart.

A dream called *us*.

The Weight of Expectations

With her results out and glowing brighter than anyone had expected, Momo should've been basking in celebration. But instead, the weight of *what now?* settled on her chest like a rock. Relatives flooded in—some physically, most digitally.

"What's next?"

"MBA? MTech? Or something better?"

"We hope you're not wasting time on that drawing-writing stuff."

The very things that helped her survive—sketching, journaling, writing letters to herself—were now labelled *timepass*.

She smiled politely, but inside, she screamed.

Her father brought up government exams. Her mother worried about marriage proposals.

And somewhere in that chaos, Dudu remained her constant. Not loud. Not imposing. Just *there*—like a lighthouse, quietly guiding her through stormy waters.

One night, Momo broke down.

Momo: *"I feel like I don't belong to myself anymore. Everyone wants a piece of me for their plans. But what about mine?"*

Dudu listened in silence, and then gently said:

Dudu: *"You know what's worse than failing? Living someone else's version of success."*

She sniffled.

Momo: *"But I don't even know what I want anymore."*

Dudu: *"That's okay. Not knowing is a sign you're still* *discovering. Don't rush it."*

Their calls became therapy. He didn't try to fix things. He just held space for her, letting her untangle her mind one thread at a time.

And amid all the confusion, one night he asked softly, "Momo, if the world didn't pressure you... what would you choose?"

She didn't even think.

"I'd write. I'd dance. I'd travel. I'd... just breathe."

He smiled through the call.

"Then maybe, one step at a time, we'll build that life together. Yours. Not theirs."

Momo didn't know what the future held. But in that moment, she knew one thing: She wasn't alone in this war between dreams and expectations.

And sometimes, that was enough to fight a little harder.

Quiet Rebellions and Secret Dreams

While the world thought Momo was preparing for a respectable government exam or plotting her MBA path, she was doing something wildly scandalous by society's standards—

She was dreaming.

Dreaming of a life with color, chaos, and creation.

With Dudu's gentle nudges and unwavering support, she started applying to fellowships, content writing jobs, even open mic poetry nights. She dusted off her sketches, rewrote her old poems, and even submitted a short story to a magazine.

She didn't tell anyone—not even her closest friends.

Because some dreams need silence to grow, away from the noise of judgment.

Dudu became her secret co-conspirator. He edited her stories, helped her rehearse her poems, and once stayed up all night helping her fill a form she had almost given up on.

Dudu: *"You're not just talented, Momo. You're brave. Braver than anyone sees."*

Her confidence started returning in small sparks. One day, she received an email:

"**Congratulations, your piece has been selected for publication.**"

She sat frozen for a second, then screamed into her pillow—half joy, half disbelief. Dudu called immediately.

Dudu: *"I told you. They saw what I've always seen."*

But the best part?

It wasn't the recognition.

It was the realization that she could make her own choices, carve her own path—quietly, steadily, rebelliously.

Every time her relatives spoke of bank exams, she smiled politely. But inside, she was building her own empire, brick by passionate brick.

She even wrote a piece titled:

"The Girl Who Smiled and Broke Traditions Silently."

It was Momo in every line.

And when she asked Dudu if it felt too bold, he said:

"Not bold. Real. And real is always worth it."

The Earthquake at the Dining Table

The house smelled of turmeric and tension.

It started like any ordinary dinner—chapatis on the plate, news humming in the background, and Momo's dad asking, *"So, how's the bank exam prep going?"*

Her hand paused mid-bite. The lie was ready on her tongue, but something in her cracked.

"I'm not doing it," she said quietly.

The spoon clattered in someone's hand.

"What do you mean you're not doing it?" her uncle asked, his voice sharper than the green chili in the sabzi.

She looked up, heart racing.

"I'm not preparing for bank or SSC or any of those. I want to write. I've been writing. And I got published."

The silence was so loud it could've shattered windows.

Her mother blinked rapidly, her cousin choked on water, and her father just stared.

"Writing?" he repeated like it was a foreign language.

"You'll earn from that? You'll make a living writing *poems*?"

The mockery stung more than the disbelief.

Momo didn't cry. She didn't scream. She just sat there,

breathing through the chaos. Then quietly added, "I already earned my first payment."

That was the real earthquake. And not a single person knew how to handle the aftershocks. They called her crazy, irresponsible, even selfish.

But Momo didn't flinch. Not this time.

Because that morning, Dudu had said something that clung to her ribs like armor:

"Let them shout. They'll get tired. But your dreams? They'll wait forever, if they have to."

She spent the night on the terrace, alone under the stars. And for the first time in forever, she felt *free*.

Broken, bruised, but free.

The Leap of Faith

The train ticket felt heavier than her entire suitcase.

Momo had never traveled alone before—not this far, not for *herself*. But the creative writing workshop in Delhi was calling her louder than any syllabus or society ever had.

She hadn't told anyone at home the real reason behind the trip. To them, it was just another "career guidance seminar." But her heart knew—it was her escape plan. Her chance to breathe.

The night before the journey, she called Dudu.

"Are you scared?" he asked softly. She didn't lie this time. **"Terrified."**

He chuckled. **"Then it's worth it."**

Morning came wrapped in nervous energy. Her bag was packed, her notebook tucked in like a good- luck charm. At the station, she was early—too early. And anxious.

But then—she saw him.

Standing by the tea stall, hands in pockets, eyes scanning the crowd.

Dudu.

Momo blinked, unsure if she was dreaming.

He walked over, casually, like he did this every day.

"You didn't think I'd let you go on your first solo trip without a

proper see-off, did you?"

She wanted to cry. Instead, she just laughed and hit his arm. They stood there, sharing chai and silence, while the platform buzzed with strangers and announcements. It felt unreal. Like the universe had paused for them.

When the train arrived, she hesitated.

"What if I fail?" she whispered.

Dudu leaned in, his voice firm and warm.

"Then you'll fail with courage. And next time, you'll rise with fire."

As the train pulled away, she watched him fade into the distance—but his words stayed, louder than ever.

Momo was no longer just a girl with scars. She was a girl in motion.

The Space Between Us

Delhi changed her.

Not in the loud, dramatic way movies show. But quietly. Like rain soaking into soil—slow, deep, and lasting.

Momo came back with new pages in her notebook, a spark in her eyes, and a little more steel in her spine.

But the moment she stepped off the train, something felt...off. Dudu wasn't there.

She had told herself not to expect him—he was busy, life happens, maybe he couldn't make it. But her heart had waited anyway.

And now it sank.

The next few days were strange.

He replied to her messages. Short ones. Dry ones.

"Hope your workshop went well." "Busy with classes. We'll talk soon."

But "soon" kept slipping further away.

Momo didn't panic. Not yet. Maybe he was just tired. Maybe *she* was being too clingy. Maybe everything was fine and her mind was just playing its old games again.

But the ache grew.

That familiar ache of silence. The one that had once hollowed her out. She called him late one night.

No answer.

The next day, he finally picked up.

"Sorry. Things have been hectic. I just... needed some space."

That word hit harder than she expected.

"Space?" she asked quietly.

"Just for a while. Nothing's wrong. I just... don't want to say the wrong thing and hurt you."

Momo swallowed the lump in her throat.

"Too late for that."

That night, she wrote in her journal:

He was the one who taught me to breathe again. And now he's the air I can't reach.

She didn't cry. Not yet.

Because part of her still believed he'd come back.

Maybe not tomorrow. Maybe not with flowers.

But with the same eyes that once saw her when she was invisible.

Until then, she waited—not like a damsel, but like a storm held in pause.

The Distance That Spoke Louder

Days turned into weeks.

Momo stopped checking her phone first thing in the morning. Not because she didn't care, but because she couldn't afford to shatter every sunrise with disappointment.

The "good morning" texts had stopped. The late-night calls had faded into memory. All that remained was a silence so loud, it echoed in her bones.

But this time, she didn't let it break her. She picked up her pen. She poured every unanswered message, every paused sentence, every emotion she couldn't speak into words that finally made sense on paper. Her journal pages were no longer just scribbles—they were her therapy, her voice, her protest against the silence.

Her mentor noticed the shift.

"Momo, your writing feels... raw. Real. What changed?"

She smiled faintly.

"I stopped writing for attention. I started writing to survive."

Meanwhile, Dudu was fighting a battle of his own.

His career was on the edge—interviews, thesis reviews, job pressure, sleepless nights. But more than that, he was scared. Scared of hurting her with his own instability. Scared of losing her while trying to protect her from his mess.

So, he distanced himself. Not because he didn't care. But because he cared too much and didn't know how to show it right.

It was a rainy Thursday when he finally called. Momo's heart skipped.
She picked up after the second ring.

"Momo..."
His voice cracked a little.

"I've been stupid. I thought pushing you away would protect you. I didn't realise I was just... hurting you more."

There was silence. Heavy, loaded.

"Why didn't you just say that?"

"Because I was afraid you'd leave if you saw how lost I was."

Momo breathed in deeply.

"I would've stayed. I was already there."

That night, they didn't promise forever.
They didn't speak in poetry or grand gestures.
They just stayed on the call for hours—talking, breathing, healing.
And somewhere between "Are you eating properly?" and "I missed your laugh," something broken quietly began to mend.

The Rain That Reunited Them

It was an ordinary day.

The sky was cloudy, the wind moody, and Momo was standing outside her PG gate, clutching her bag tightly, waiting for an auto. Her mind was busy untangling thoughts about an upcoming exam, when suddenly—

A familiar voice cut through the breeze.

"Need a ride?"

She turned.

There he was.

Dudu. Standing in front of a black scooty. Helmet in hand. Eyes... searching hers. For a second, she forgot how to breathe.

"What are you doing here?" she finally managed.

"Came to see if the girl I almost lost still wants to talk to me."

Momo didn't speak. She walked past him, opened the scooty seat, placed her bag gently inside, sat sideways like she always did—and looked at him.

"Let's go."

That one word. That one moment. It melted everything.

They didn't talk for the first ten minutes of the ride. The wind did the talking. Her dupatta fluttered behind her like a quiet surrender. His eyes stayed on the road, but his heart was crashing against his ribs.

When they finally stopped, it wasn't at a café, or a park. It was at the same agricultural department where they'd once had their first deep conversation.
History repeating, but with softer hearts.

They sat on the same old bench.
Rain started to drizzle—just like that day. Dudu finally spoke.

"I thought I needed to be perfect to love you right. But now I know... I just needed to be honest."

Momo turned to him. Her voice was low, but firm.

"And I thought I needed to be quiet to keep you. But I've learned... silence only creates more distance."

They looked at each other.
There were no grand confessions. No apologies rehearsed. Just truth. Raw and awkward. But real.

As the rain grew heavier, Dudu removed his hoodie and gently covered Momo's head with it. She laughed softly.

"You never change."

"Neither do you," he said, smiling. "Still too stubborn to carry an umbrella."

They laughed. Together this time.

And in that moment, beneath that shared hoodie, soaked clothes, messy hair and teary eyes, something clicked back into place.

Not just love.

But understanding.

Notes, Nerves, and Never-Ending Support

The final exams were around the corner.
Momo's desk looked like a war zone—notes scattered, sticky tabs hanging like limp flags, coffee
stains marking territories of stress. Sleep was a luxury, time was a thief, and pressure was at its peak. But this time... she wasn't alone.

Every morning started with the same ritual.

Dudu's text at 6:45 AM sharp:

"Good morning, topper. Time to show the books who's boss."
And every night ended with his voice, calm and comforting, saying,

"You've got this, Momo. I believe in you more than you believe in Newton's laws."

Even though he wasn't physically around all the time, his presence lingered in little things.
— The tiffin that magically arrived during lunch breaks, always with her favourite food and a sticky note that said, *"Fuel for the fighter."*
— The photocopies of important notes that showed up at her PG

gate just when she needed them the most.

— The motivational audio clips he'd send when she looked extra drained in their video calls. Sometimes it was a quote, sometimes a joke, and once, even a silly rap:

"Momo the mighty, stressed but brighty, gonna kill the exam like a queen all flighty."

She had laughed for the first time that week.

One evening, while revising a particularly tricky topic, her eyes welled up. It wasn't about the syllabus. It was the fear of failing him, failing herself, falling short of the version he believed in.

She called him.

No words. Just silence.

And then, his voice:

"You don't have to prove anything to me. You just have to be you. That's always been more than enough."

She wiped her tears and got back to studying.

Finally, the exam week arrived.

On Day 1, as she stepped out of her PG, she found a tiny box tied to her scooty handle. Inside was a gel pen, a tiny paper scroll, and a candy.

The scroll read:

"Write your future with this, sweeten your soul with this, and remember—my heart is always with you. Love, Dudu."

And she did. Paper after paper, she poured her heart into the answers. Every time she felt like giving up, she thought of him—his faith, his warmth, his presence.

He didn't just support her academically. He reminded her of her worth when she forgot it. He helped her breathe when pressure suffocated her.

Together, they weren't just surviving the final exams. They were conquering them.

The Results of Love

The last exam ended with the rustle of papers and a collective sigh across the hall. Students rushed out like free birds, laughing, planning parties, making calls. But Momo... just stood still for a moment, breathing it all in.

It was over.

The pressure. The panic. The endless nights.

She walked out slowly, her legs heavy from exhaustion, but her heart? Light. Because this time, she wasn't just proud of herself—she was grateful. For the silent strength that stood behind her every step of the way.

And then, there he was.

Leaning against his scooty outside the gate, arms crossed, sunglasses on, looking like her personal bodyguard and proudest fan in one frame. No flowers. No balloons. Just a quiet smile that said, *"You did it."*

Momo ran up to him, dropped her bag like it held all her stress, and threw her arms around him. He chuckled softly. "Result toh aana baaki hai..."

She pulled back just a little and said, "But *I* know I've already won."

He touched her forehead with his gently, a gesture they had grown into—quiet, soft, intimate.

"I'm proud of you, Momo. Not just for the exams... but for surviving everything that tried to break you."

He took her to a quiet spot, a little hill behind the college where the city lights blinked in the distance.

There was a small setup—two folding chairs, a thermos of coffee, and a container of her favourite biryani.

She looked at him, wide-eyed. "What is this?"

He shrugged, trying to act casual. "A post-exam therapy session. Doctor Dudu prescribes food, fresh air, and forehead kisses."

She laughed—genuinely, freely, for the first time in days.

They ate under the stars, shared stories about the most ridiculous MCQs in the exams, and even argued over who would have scored higher if he had written the same paper.

Spoiler: she still said *herself.*

As the night deepened and the air turned cooler, he wrapped his jacket around her and whispered, "Exams done. Pressure over. And now... it's time to dream again. Together."

She nodded, snuggling into the warmth of his jacket—and his love. And in that quiet, cozy moment, Momo realized...

Final exams weren't just about marks.

They were about learning who stays when the going gets tough.

And Dudu?

He didn't just stay.

He stood beside her like a wall.

A wall that whispered love through silence, food, notes, and forehead kisses.

The Rank That Rocked Their World

The result day arrived with a mix of hope, fear, and oddly... peace.

Momo woke up early, even before the birds. Her phone buzzed with group chats exploding— screenshots, roll numbers, cries, celebrations.

But she didn't check.

Not yet.

Instead, she stood in front of her mirror, looking at the girl who had once been broken... who had once cried herself to sleep, unsure if she was enough.

And now?

She was about to find out.

When she finally opened the website, her fingers trembled. She typed her roll number with slow precision, every digit echoing in her chest.

Click. Loading... And then... **AIR 8**

She blinked.

Refreshed the page.

Looked again.

AIR 8.

Not just passed.

Not just a topper.

A freakin' national-level rank holder.

She stared at the screen, tears blurring the numbers. Not because she doubted herself. But because this—*this*—was the moment everything changed.

She called Dudu.

No words.

Just a choked whisper, "Check the result..." He didn't even ask her rank.

He knew.

He reached her place in fifteen minutes, breathless, hair all messed up, face glowing like he had won the rank himself.

"Momo... *you did it.*"

"No... *we* did it," she said, holding up her hand for a high-five that melted into a hug.

It wasn't a Bollywood-style celebration. No music. No crowd. Just two people who knew the weight of every sacrifice, every sleepless night, every emotional breakdown.

And the beauty of healing together.

Later that evening, the college group chat had blown up. Everyone was talking about the girl who used to sit alone, sketch in corners, eat quietly, avoid eye contact...

Now, she was *The Momo.* The ranker. The achiever.

Dudu's colleagues sent him congratulatory messages. "Your student made you proud, sir." He just smiled.

Because she was never *just* a student.

That night, they sat under the same tree where he once found her crying after her first assignment. Only this time, the tears were different.

"I'm scared," she admitted. "Of what?"

"Of what's next. What if I lose myself?"

He held her hand tightly. "Then I'll remind you. Every single day, how far you've come. And who you are."

And in that moment, Momo understood something deeper than results and ranks. She hadn't just topped an exam.

She had conquered her trauma. And Dudu?

He wasn't just her mentor or her love. He was her anchor.

When Whispers Turned into Theories

The college was buzzing.

Not with academic stress or assignment deadlines—no. This was *tea time*, but not the kind you drink. It started subtly.

A junior spotted Momo walking across the corridor, and Dudu passed by from the other side. Their eyes met for a brief second—a quick exchange, nothing dramatic.

But to a gossip-hungry college crowd? That was *everything.*

"She smiled at him. Did you see that?"

"And he smiled back... bro, not his usual professional smile. This one had sparkle." "Don't be dumb. Maybe she's just grateful—he taught her and all."

"Grateful with sparkles?" Boom. The theory was born.

One day, during a lecture, Dudu absentmindedly said, "Like Momo explained in her assignment..."

Pin-drop silence.

"Sir... how do you know what *Momo* wrote?" one of the more daring boys asked with a sly grin. Dudu coughed. "I meant... Momo... she had asked a doubt. I remember it from there."

A very awkward sip from his water bottle followed. The class didn't buy it.

Meanwhile, Momo started getting strange looks in the library.

Girls leaned in to whisper as she passed by. Boys smiled too wide.

One even dared to ask, "Hey Momo, are you giving *extra tuition* to sir?"

She replied with the deadliest straight face, "Yeah. In how to tolerate idiots." Silence. Victory.

But the gossip didn't stop.

It reached a whole new level when someone saw Dudu waiting near the staff room... holding a lunchbox.

And later, Momo's friend posted a blurry boomerang of *someone* handing over *something* to Dudu under a tree.

The caption?

"Love is in the air... or is that just biryani?"

Comments exploded.

Dudu, usually calm and composed, finally lost it one day.

"Do these kids have no syllabus? Why are they trying to be CID agents?" Momo laughed for ten minutes straight.

"But we *are* a little obvious now," she teased.

"Oh, really? Next time I'll just walk past you without blinking."

"You've tried. You looked like you were having a seizure."

Touché.

In staff meetings, things got even juicier.

One of the female professors chuckled, "Sir, your student's quite the star nowadays." Dudu just nodded, sipping tea like a scandal-free saint.

But Momo knew.

Behind that expressionless face was a man enjoying every bit of the madness.

Their story was still a secret. But secrets?
They're like perfume.
You can hide the bottle, but the scent always lingers.

The Night of Lights and Silent Confessions

It was the final event of the year—the college farewell function. Lights draped the entrance like stars had fallen just for one night. Music echoed from the auditorium. Students dressed in their flashiest ethnic fits, phones buzzing with reels and selfies. Emotions? High.

But Momo?

She was nervous.

Not about her outfit or makeup. But about *him*. Would he come? Would he notice?

Would she be able to hide the storm inside her?

She walked in with her gang, wearing a deep maroon saree—elegant, bold, mature. Her usual giggles were toned down. Her eyes? Searching.

And then... There he was.

Standing near the stage in a navy blue blazer, crisp white shirt, and that signature watch she secretly adored. His hair was combed back, jawline sharp, expression unreadable.

But when his eyes found her? He blinked.

Once. Twice.

And then looked away, quickly. Too quickly. Momo smiled.

Gotcha.

Later, the anchor called out,

"And now, a surprise performance by... Momo and friends!"

Dudu looked up, surprised. He hadn't heard about this.
The lights dimmed. Music started. And Momo walked to center stage with a mic in her hand. Not to sing.
Not to dance.
But to *speak*.

She started:
"We all go through things in college—stress, heartbreak, confusion. But sometimes... if we're lucky... we also meet someone who sees us.
Even when we're invisible to ourselves." The crowd cheered.
But Dudu?
He froze.
Her voice was steady, her words indirect—but they hit home.
"To that 'someone'—thank you.
For standing quietly in the background. For giving light when I was lost.
For reminding me I'm not broken... just healing."
Applause.
Dudu didn't clap.
He just... stared.
And Momo walked off the stage, heart pounding.

After the event, she stood alone near the exit, pretending to scroll her phone. He passed by, alone, silent.
But this time, he didn't look away. He paused.
"Momo," he said softly. She turned. "Hmm?"
There was a flicker of hesitation in his eyes. Then... "You looked nice on stage. Spoke well."

"You too," she replied, smirking. "Stood well." That earned a low chuckle.

Silence followed. Comfortable. Heavy. Real. He wanted to say more. She could feel it.

But instead, he said—

"Let's go. It's getting late."

And just like that, he walked beside her. No holding hands. No dramatic confessions. Just... presence.

And sometimes, that's louder than love.

Rain, Roads, and Realizations

College was over.

Assignments were done. Farewell was behind them.

But one thing remained—a last trip. A getaway planned by the seniors for memories, photos, and that final dose of madness before life moved on.

And yes—Momo was going. So was Dudu.

But no one knew they'd be seated next to each other on the bus.

Totally accidental.

Totally unforgettable.

The journey began with chaos—snacks, speakers, screaming, dance-offs in the aisle.

But Momo had her earphones in, head resting lightly on the window, eyes watching the sky blur past.

Dudu sat beside her, silent, occasionally glancing her way.

He wanted to say something. But words didn't come easy today.

After a while, she whispered, without looking, "You're thinking too loud."

He chuckled. "You're quiet." She smirked, "You're nosy."

And just like that, the wall cracked.

They reached a hill station by evening. Misty weather. Pine trees. A cozy resort. Rooms were allotted randomly. But Momo's was right opposite Dudu's.

Coincidence?

Let's pretend it was.

They explored the market, clicked photos, tried momos (because obviously), and laughed under fairy lights.

It felt light. Uncomplicated. Until the **rain** came.

Back at the resort, it poured. Everyone huddled around a bonfire inside the hall. Momo sat near the window, watching raindrops race. Dudu approached quietly. "Can I?" he asked, pointing to the seat beside her.

She nodded.

They sat in silence, watching the rain dance. Then... softly... she spoke.

"Do you ever feel like... you're finally okay... but then something small happens, and you spiral back?" He didn't answer immediately.

Then:

"Yes. Often.

Healing's not a straight road. It's a roundabout." She smiled faintly. "You're wiser in the rain."

He turned to her. "You're softer in the quiet." Their eyes met.

That night, as everyone slept, Momo sat on the balcony in her hoodie. The rain had stopped. The wind was cold.

Suddenly, her phone buzzed.

Dudu: "You okay?"

She replied: "Couldn't sleep." A pause.

Then:

Dudu: "Want to talk?" She looked up.

There he was—across the corridor, leaning on his balcony too. No words.

Just a shared moment in the silence of the night. Two souls. Two balconies. One connection.

Truth or Dare, Heart or Hide

The night wasn't over.

Someone shouted, "**TRUTH OR DARE!**"

And of course, the whole group got dragged in.

A big circle. A flickering bonfire. Echoes of laughter.

Everyone knew the drill—no skipping, no lies, no mercy.

Momo sat with her knees pulled close, next to her closest friends.

Dudu sat diagonally across the circle—calm, composed, but very much *aware* of her.

The bottle spun wildly, stopping at people who were made to propose trees, mimic teachers, or confess first crushes.

Then, it stopped on **Momo**.

"Truth or dare?" someone grinned. She thought for a second. "Truth."

Her friend smirked. "Okay, tell us... *who in this room has your heart right now?*"

The air shifted.

Everyone went "Ooooh!"

Momo blinked. Froze. Laughed nervously.

"Next question, please."

"No skipping!" they all shouted. She exhaled, cheeks glowing red. Her eyes didn't move.

They didn't have to.

They drifted toward the quiet, steady boy across the fire. Dudu.

He didn't smile.

He didn't react.

But his eyes—*they softened.* The bottle spun again.

And guess who it landed on next?

Dudu.

Everyone roared. "Come on, Professor! Truth or dare?" He leaned forward slightly, eyes still on Momo.

"Truth."

A boy smirked, "Okay... have you ever fallen for someone younger than you?" Gasps. Laughter.

Momo's heart stopped.

He looked around.

Then answered calmly. "Yes."

And he didn't look at anyone... Except her.

After the game ended, people scattered—some to their rooms, some to midnight snacks. Momo stepped out for air. The stars were out.

Footsteps behind her. Dudu.

He walked beside her in silence, hands in his pockets.

"About that question," she whispered, without turning, "Was it true?"

He didn't reply immediately.

Then he stopped walking.

"If I lied, would that make you feel safer?" "And if I told the truth... would it scare you?"

She stopped too.

"It already did both."

They looked at each other—two people, two different ages, two different worlds. And yet... something undeniable.

He smiled softly.

"I didn't plan any of this, Momo. But you... happened."

And in that moment, under the stars, something shifted. Not love. Not yet.

But something that *felt* like the start of it.

The Caretaker

The trip was over.

Bags were packed, buses loaded, sleepy faces leaned on windows, and everyone prepared to head back to routine.

Momo, however, wasn't the same girl who had come on this trip. Something had changed.

She wasn't confused anymore. She *knew* what she felt.

And even if words hadn't been said, the glances, silences, and that starry night had said more than enough.

On the bus ride back, Momo kept glancing at the front seat. Dudu sat there, unusually quiet.

Usually, he'd be the one reading, managing, or lightly smiling at the chaos around. But today—he just rested his head back, eyes closed, brows slightly furrowed.

Something was off.

A few hours in, he stood up to get water and stumbled a bit. Momo saw it.

She immediately got up and walked toward him. "Are you okay?" He gave a weak smile. "Yeah... just a little tired."

But she touched his forehead—burning.

"You have a fever," she whispered. "Sit. Don't argue."

She took the seat beside him and started rummaging through her bag for medicine.

Someone else would've been shocked—*Momo*, the shy, stubborn, quiet girl, bossing *him* around? But Dudu just obeyed. He closed his eyes again, resting against the window.

She handed him water, medicine, and gently adjusted his scarf. For once, he let someone take care of him.

"You're not used to this, are you?" she said quietly. "Being looked after."

He opened one eye and gave a faint smile. "Not really."

She didn't say anything after that.

She just placed her hand over his, her thumb gently tracing circles. For hours, she sat like that—half-worried, half-proud, fully in love. As the bus neared the college, he stirred and said, "Thank you." "For the medicine?" she teased.

"No.

For... making me feel like I matter. Like I'm not alone."

She didn't respond.

But her silence said everything.

After they got off the bus, she made sure he reached his room safely, even got some food packed for him.

Later that night, a message popped up on her phone.

Dudu: You looked after me better than I've ever looked after myself. She smiled.

Typed back.

Momo: Good. Now you know what it feels like to have someone who cares. Get used to it. I'm not going anywhere.

The Unspeakable Something

Back at college, everything resumed—assignments, classes, late-night submissions, sleepy lectures. But for Momo and Dudu, *nothing* felt the same.

Their bond had shifted—something unspoken was blooming between them, stretching beyond friendship, beyond gratitude, beyond words. And yet... they said nothing.

No "I love you." No "I need you."

Just glances, late-night calls, and subtle gestures that screamed the truth.

One afternoon, while Momo was sitting under the neem tree near the library, scrolling through photos from the trip, she paused on *that* one.

The one where Dudu stood alone on the bridge, hands in pockets, looking up at the sky.

She hadn't taken that photo. Someone else had. But it captured something she hadn't seen before. He looked... soft.

Peaceful.

Almost like *he* had finally found something he wasn't searching for. Her phone buzzed.

Dudu: Class at 4. Don't be late, sleepyhead. She smirked.

Momo: I won't if *someone* doesn't give me night-long lectures on heartbreaks and healing.

Dudu: Guilty.

There it was again—this teasing, this comfort, this slow dance of emotions.

In class, she noticed how he looked at her now. Not directly. Not obviously.

But every time she answered a question, every time she smiled at someone, his eyes lingered just a bit longer.

After class, as students filed out, he called her name softly. "Momo."

She turned. "Yeah?"

He paused. Then changed his mind. "Never mind. Just... you're doing good."

She gave him a look—half smile, half confusion. "You're weird."

"So are you," he replied.

And that was the end of it—for now.

That night, while on call, they were both quiet.

Breaths and silence. The kind that didn't need to be filled.

Suddenly, she said—"You ever feel like... something is about to change?" He didn't answer immediately.

Then—

"Every time I talk to you." Her heart skipped.

But she played it cool. "Smooth."

He chuckled. "I try."

They didn't say it that night. No confessions. No promises.

Just the feeling. The unspeakable something. Growing.

Brewing. Waiting.

When Silence Speaks Louder

It was just another day. Or so they thought.

Classes were done, and the corridor buzzed with the usual chaos—students laughing, rushing, living. But Dudu was quiet. Too quiet.

Momo noticed it instantly. He wasn't joking around. He wasn't teasing. He wasn't even correcting anyone's grammar—his favourite pastime.

She caught up with him near the staff room.

"Hey, everything okay?" He gave a small nod. "Just tired."

But Momo had known him long enough by now to read between the lines.

This wasn't tired. This was twisted-up-inside, something-on-his-mind, distracted Dudu.

"Wanna talk?"

He looked at her for a beat.

And then, without saying a word, he started walking. She followed.

They ended up on the terrace of the library building. Windy. Isolated. Quiet.

They both leaned against the railing, looking at the orange sky folding into twilight.

"Why do we always end up in these dramatic filmy locations?" she joked, trying to lighten the mood. "Maybe because we are the drama," he replied, his voice soft.

Silence again.

Then, he spoke.

"Momo... what are we?"

The question dropped like thunder between them. She blinked. Heart pounding.

"I mean..." he continued, "I know we're friends. But there's more, right? Or is it just me?" Momo felt everything freeze.

And then melt.

In the same second.

"It's not just you," she whispered. That was it.

That's all it took.

The world didn't change.

But *theirs* did.

He smiled—finally, a real one.

"Good. Because I don't think I can keep pretending."

Momo stepped closer. "Me neither."

They didn't hug. They didn't kiss. They just stood there, side by side, fingers brushing slightly. A silent agreement. A quiet confession.

Sometimes love doesn't need big declarations. Sometimes, it just *is*.

Not a Date (But Totally a Date)

The next few days were a beautiful mess of nervousness and excitement. They still met every day.

Still talked every night. Still shared everything.

But now, there was an *unspoken something* in the air. A softness in his voice.

A skip in her heartbeat.

They hadn't officially labeled it. But something had changed. And everyone could see it—even the canteen bhaiya, who smirked when he saw them together.

Then one afternoon, Dudu messaged:

"Let's go out. Just us. You and me. Sunday?" Momo blinked at the screen.

Butterflies? No—*a whole zoo.*

She typed and deleted at least six replies before settling on: "Okay. Where?"

He replied instantly.

"Somewhere simple. Not fancy. Just... us."

Sunday arrived.

Momo wore the yellow kurti Dudu once said made her look like "sunshine on caffeine." She didn't overdo the makeup. Just kajal, lip balm, and the secret weapon: her smile.

He was already waiting near the main gate, looking effortlessly good in a simple shirt and jeans. Casual, but... *heart-thief level.*

"You're late," he said, pretending to frown. "You're early," she teased back.

"I was excited," he mumbled.

They went to a little cafe near the lake—tiny tables, fairy lights, and old Bollywood songs humming in the background.

It wasn't about the food.

It wasn't even about the place.

It was about *being there*. Together.

They laughed. Talked about random things. Made fun of each other. And every time their hands brushed, it felt like tiny fireworks.

Halfway through, Momo asked:

"So... is this a date?"

Dudu looked at her for a second, then smiled. "Only if you want it to be."

She smiled back. "Then yeah... it is."

And just like that, it became their first unofficial, almost awkward, heartwarmingly perfect *official*

date.

No labels. No pressure.

Just Momo and Dudu, figuring it out together.

The First Crack

After the dreamy not-a-date that totally was, Momo felt like she was floating. But love... even the purest kind... comes with its shadows.

And that shadow arrived faster than either of them expected. It started small.

A missed call.

A late reply.

A message seen but not responded to.

Dudu was caught up in something—college work, perhaps—but Momo didn't know that. All she knew was that her texts were being left on read.

Her mind, like always, ran wild.

"He's getting bored of me." *"Maybe I was too much."*

"Or maybe he realized I'm not good enough."

Insecurity wrapped itself around her like a blanket she couldn't shake off.

When Dudu finally called at night, cheerful and calm, she couldn't hold it in anymore. "Where were you the whole day?" her voice was sharp. "You ignored my texts." "Momo... I was in a meeting. I told you yesterday—"

"You could've replied. One word. One emoji even." "I didn't think it would upset you this much."

"Well, it did!" Silence.

Then he softly asked, "Do you really think I'd ignore you on purpose?" Momo bit her lip. Her anger was never about the delay. It was the fear.

Fear of losing the only person who ever saw her whole and loved her anyway. "No," she whispered. "I'm sorry. I just... I overthink. I always ruin good things." Dudu sighed, not out of irritation, but concern.

"You don't ruin things, Momo. You just... get scared. And that's okay. But promise me something?" "What?"

"Next time your mind goes crazy, talk to me. Don't fight me. I'm not going anywhere." Tears welled up in her eyes. Not of sadness, but relief.

"Okay," she said.

Their first fight wasn't loud or cruel. It wasn't a storm. It was a mirror—reflecting the fears they both carried.

And in choosing to talk instead of walk away, they only grew stronger.

Proof in the Little Things

The morning after their argument, Momo woke up with a heavy heart and puffy eyes. She had barely slept, thinking about Dudu—replaying every word, every pause, every sigh from the night before.

Her phone buzzed.

"Check your gate." – *Dudu*

Confused, she rushed to the front gate of her house. Her heart skipped a beat.

There it was. A little white box wrapped with a ribbon, sitting on the floor like it had traveled miles just to comfort her.

Inside, she found—

Her favorite chocolate bar, A tiny hand-written note,

And a Polaroid of the two of them—laughing, carefree, from the day they met in the canteen. The note read:

"Momo,

Arguments don't scare me. Silence does.

So talk. Cry. Overthink. Just don't shut me out. I'm here. Even when I'm not near.

– Your Dudu"

She clutched the note to her chest. The tears came again, but this time, they were warm. She called him instantly.

"You came all the way here?" she asked, voice trembling. "I just had to prove something."

"Prove what?"

"That no distance, no argument, no overthinking will ever make me love you less." She couldn't speak. She didn't have to. Her silence was soaked in love this time.

That day, Momo understood something she had only heard in movies before—

Real love isn't in butterflies or fairytales.

It's in staying, showing up, and sending chocolates after a fight.
And with that, the crack in their story?
It turned into a window—letting in more light than ever before.

The Dance of Dreams

With exams finally over and their bond stronger than ever, Momo and Dudu found themselves with a little more breathing space, a little more time to dream—and most importantly, time to live.

One lazy Sunday afternoon, Momo was curled up in bed scrolling through dance videos. The way the dancers moved with passion and freedom reminded her of something she had tucked away— her love for dancing.

Dudu called right then, as if he sensed the thought in her mind. "Kya dekh rahi ho, Momo?"

"Dance videos... bas aise hi," she replied softly. "Toh phir kar lo na... You're made for it."

"Kab? Kahan? Kaise?"

"Mere saamne. Abhi. Call pe. I'll watch." She laughed, half shocked, half shy. "Pagal ho kya?"

"Haan, tumhare liye."

That line alone was enough to flip her hesitation into fire. She got up, played a song, and began to dance—barefoot, hair messy, no makeup, no filters. Just her, and the music, and Dudu watching silently on the other side of the screen.

When she finished, out of breath and blushing, he was still speechless. "Momo... tumne mujhe firse pyaar sikha diya."

She bit her lip, smiling like a child who had just shown off her secret treasure. "You think I should try again? Like... take it seriously?"

"I think the world needs to see what I see."

That day, they sat for hours making a plan—Momo would start posting small clips, maybe open a YouTube channel, even attend a dance workshop. Dudu would help with editing and captions. It wasn't just her dream anymore; now it was their project.

In between, they'd tease each other, argue over song choices, laugh over bloopers, and celebrate even the smallest likes or comments.

And every night, Dudu would remind her:

"You've always been magic. I'm just helping you see it."

That chapter wasn't about a grand gesture or dramatic twist.

It was about belief. About two people turning a quiet passion into a shared purpose.

And for the first time, Momo didn't just dream with her eyes closed... She danced with them wide open.

Shadows of Silence

The silence after the last conversation between Momo and Dudu was heavier than anything she'd
felt before. Not the silence that brings peace, but the kind that screams louder than words. Days had passed since they last spoke like they used to. The long calls, the random good morning messages, the way he would tease her just to hear her pout—it had all vanished into an uncomfortable pause.

Momo's heart wasn't quiet, though. It rumbled with questions. Was he pulling away? Was she too much? Or maybe... maybe he had grown tired of her presence. But deep down, a whisper inside told her otherwise—this wasn't disinterest. It was a storm. A storm he was hiding from her.

She started journaling again, this time not about her dreams but about her fears. She'd write letters to him she never sent. "I miss us," one of them began. Another ended with, "Please don't carry your burdens alone. Share them with me. I'm here... always."

On a particularly silent evening, Momo found herself standing in front of a café they both had once talked about visiting together. She stared at the empty seat on the patio and imagined Dudu there, sipping his cold coffee, smirking as he watched her over the rim of his cup. A tear rolled down, but she smiled. Because even memories were a kind of presence.

But just as she was about to leave, her phone buzzed. One message. From Dudu.

"I'm sorry for being distant. There's so much happening... and I didn't want to pull you into it. But maybe that was my mistake. Because you're the only one who could've held me through it."

Her hands trembled. This wasn't just an apology. This was a key—one unlocking all the silence, the doubt, the distance.

She replied:

"You don't have to protect me from the storm. Let me stand with you in the rain."

That night, they didn't talk much. No long conversations, no teasing. But the silence between them had changed. It was warm again. Healing.

The Final Exam and a Silent Confession

The sun of the final exam day rose with both excitement and nervousness. Momo's fingers trembled slightly as she tied her hair into a ponytail. Today wasn't just the last exam—it was the last day she'd get to see Dudu within the walls of college.

She had chosen her outfit with care. Not too flashy, but something that said *'remember me.'* Her eyes searched the crowd at the college entrance, hoping for a glimpse of him. And there he was—

standing near the gate, supervising the arrangements, his sleeves rolled up, the familiar stern look hiding the warmth only she knew.

"Momo," he called out gently as she passed him. She turned, surprised. "Yes, sir?"

"Paper 2 is a bit lengthy. Don't waste time over the first few questions." She smiled. "Thanks. I'll manage."

But what she really wanted to say was, *"Will you miss me too?"*

During the exam, her mind was half on the questions and half on him. When it ended, students poured out cheering, laughing, clicking selfies.

She stood quietly at the corridor's edge, scanning the crowd. Would he come?

And then, as if reading her thoughts, Dudu appeared. No smile, no teasing today. Just a serious face and a small gift in his hand—a book, wrapped neatly with a handwritten note.

"For you," he said. "A little something for your future." Momo opened the note later when he wasn't around.

"You're brilliant, Momo. Go make the world your canvas. And when you doubt yourself, remember: I always believed in you first."

Her eyes welled up. This wasn't just a note. This was a confession without words.

The Goodbye That Wasn't Really Goodbye

The next day was quieter. The college campus, once buzzing with exam stress, now wore the emptiness of a completed journey. Students were leaving with packed bags and heavier hearts. Some hugged, some cried, others just waved and walked away.

Momo was supposed to leave that afternoon. But something kept her lingering.

She wandered into the same corridor where she used to catch glimpses of Dudu during class breaks. The benches, the canteen, the library door—it all held echoes of moments that felt like lifetimes. Her fingers brushed against the wall near the staff room, the very spot where he once paused to ask if she was okay during her low days.

She didn't realize how long she'd been lost in her thoughts until she heard footsteps. "Momo?"

She turned around.

There he was—Dudu, standing in the same blue shirt he wore on the day they first truly spoke. "I thought you'd left," he said, voice steady but eyes uncertain.

"I wanted to," she replied, "but this place... it feels like leaving a piece of me behind." A pause.

"Maybe you should," he said softly. "Leave this part behind, but not what it gave you." Her eyes flickered. "And what about what *you* gave me?"

He looked at her for a long time. The silence wasn't empty—it was packed with everything they hadn't said out loud.

"I gave you some guidance. You... gave me something I hadn't felt in a long time," he admitted, his voice barely above a whisper.

Momo blinked. "What's that?"

"A reason to smile without pretending."

And then, as if the moment would shatter if he stayed longer, he took a step back.

"Go, Momo. Don't look back until you've done something so big that the world recognizes your name without needing an introduction."

"But what if I still want you in that world?" she asked, heart pounding. He smiled, the kind of smile that carried pain and pride at once. "Then come find me when you're done creating it."

And with that, he turned and walked away. But it wasn't the end.

It was a promise.

From Diary Pages to Dreams

Momo was back in her hometown, but nothing felt the same.

The streets, the sounds, even the sky—everything seemed to carry a question: *What now?*

Her room was as she had left it months ago, yet she wasn't the same girl anymore. The broken pieces inside her had somehow been shaped into something stronger, something softer too.

She pulled out her old diary, the one she hadn't touched since before college.

The pages were full of teenage rants, heartbreaks, and poems that felt silly now... but when she reached the middle, something changed. That's where Dudu's name started showing up—not in bold, not in capitals—but quietly. Like a whisper in a storm.

And for the first time, she didn't cry reading those pages. She smiled. It was the first real smile in days.

Days turned into weeks. She kept herself busy—wrote more, sketched again, picked up books,

danced in her room like no one was watching. But at night, she still thought of him. Of his eyes that understood too much, his silence that said more than words.

One night, after tossing and turning in bed, she sat upright and grabbed her laptop. A blank document blinked at her.

Title: The End That Began It All.

She started typing.

It wasn't just a story anymore. It was her truth, their truth.

Every moment—every high, every low, every eye contact, every unsaid thing—began to pour out like water breaking through a dam. She wrote till the sun rose. And the next night. And the next.

Within a month, Momo had a rough draft. But more than a story, she had a purpose.

She wasn't just the girl who once broke down in the washroom of her college, or the girl who had no clue where her life was heading.

She was Momo.

A girl who found her fire in the most unexpected classroom.

A Letter Never Sent

It was the first week of May again.

Exactly a year since Momo had texted him for the very first time.

Her phone buzzed with college group messages, alumni meet updates, and the usual chaos. But not from him. Dudu had gone silent. No texts, no calls, not even a "seen" on the story she'd nervously posted.

She missed him. Not the professor. Not even the friend. But the person who once saw magic in her chaos.

Sitting by the window that evening, Momo stared at the empty notepad in front of her. Then, with a deep breath, she started writing—not a diary entry this time, but a letter.

Dear Dudu,

I don't even know if I'll send this. Maybe it's just for me.

Maybe it's for that version of me who first looked at you and thought, *He's something else.*

You taught me to value myself, to look beyond scars and see strength.

You didn't just change my grades or my habits—you changed the way I saw love. You made me believe that someone could fall in love with the parts I hid.

I know we had our flaws. I know we've both been afraid. But I miss the sound of your voice, even when you said nothing at all.

If you're reading this, just know that I'll always be cheering for you. In every classroom you walk into.

In every cup of tea you sip too fast.

In every small moment that matters more than the world realizes.

Love,

Momo

She read it once. Then again. And again.

Tears fell, but they were lighter now. Like gentle rain after a long summer drought. She didn't send the letter. She didn't have to.

Writing it was enough.

And somehow, that night, she slept peacefully—for the first time in weeks. Because closure didn't always come from a reply. Sometimes, it came from finally saying what your heart had been whispering all along.

The Beginning That Never Ended

The sun was setting on another June evening.

Momo stood at the edge of the terrace, the same place where she used to cry herself to sleep, where doubts once echoed louder than dreams. But today... it felt different. Lighter. Braver. She was no longer the girl who waited to be chosen. She had become the woman who chose herself—and everything that came with her.

Her phone vibrated.

"Congratulations, Momo. Your book has been published."

She blinked twice. The notification stared back, real and shimmering.

Her story. *Their* story. Now alive in pages, waiting to be read, to be felt, to be remembered. She scrolled through the dedication page again, heart racing:

To the one who taught me how to love without words, and heal without promises. To Dudu—wherever life takes you, you'll always be my favorite chapter.

A soft knock on the door pulled her back from the screen. It was her mom.

Beta, someone's here to meet you... Momo frowned. "Who?"

Her mom simply smiled, eyes glinting with a secret she wouldn't reveal.

As Momo walked to the living room, heart pacing and hands cold, she saw him. Dudu. Standing there. Taller than she remembered. Tired eyes. But glowing, still. She froze.

He stepped forward with a shy smile—the same one she had once fallen for, back when he was just a professor with too much work and too little time.

"I read your book," he said softly.

She looked at him, still in disbelief. "You did?"

He nodded. "Every word. Every pause. Every unsent letter." Silence stretched between them like a delicate thread.

Then, he reached into his bag and pulled out a book. Her book.

And on the first page, right below the title, he had scribbled something.

To Momo — the girl who turned my ordinary life into poetry.

She bit her lip, tears pooling in her eyes. "So... what now?" He smiled.

"Now?" He looked around, then at her. "Now we write the next chapter. Together."

Outside, the wind whispered through the trees. Some love stories don't end.

They pause.

They grow.

They wait.

And then, one day, they find their way back—older, wiser, softer. Like Momo and Dudu.

Not perfect. But real.

And sometimes... that's more than enough.

THE END

(or maybe... just the beginning.)

Special Thanks

To my Drankan panda(Dudu) —

Thank you for seeing something in me when I couldn't see it in myself. For being the calm in my storms, the voice of reason in my chaos, and the faith I never knew I needed. You weren't just a chapter in my story—you were the turning point.

For every time you believed in me, pushed me, supported me, and stood silently behind the scenes cheering me on... this book is not just written for you—it's because of you.

You didn't just teach me physics. You taught me how to love.